Chicken Little

Once upon a time, there was a sweet hen named Chicken Little. She lived on a shady lane in a quiet kingdom, close to all of her friends.

One day, as Chicken Little walked past a big oak tree, a strong gust of wind rustled the branches. An acorn was blown loose, and it fell right on Chicken Little's head. It gave her quite a scare!

"The sky is falling!" squawked Chicken Little. "The sky is falling! I must tell the king—he'll know what to do!"

And so Chicken Little ran down the lane, toward the king's castle.

Along the way, Chicken Little met her friend Henny Penny.

"Hello, Chicken Little," said Henny Penny. "Why are you in such a hurry?"

"The sky is falling!" Chicken Little replicd. "I'm going to tell the king!"

Could the sky really fall? Henny Penny wasn't so sure about this.

"How do you know the sky is falling?" asked Henny Penny.

"I felt a piece of it clonk me on the head!" said Chicken Little.

"That's terrible!" Henny Penny clucked. "You're right, we must tell the king!"

Chicken Little and Henny Penny hurried down the lane, and soon saw Turkey Lurkey.

"Slow down!" said Turkey Lurkey. "Where are you dashing off to?"

"The sky is falling!" Henny Penny said. "Chicken Little told me."

"I felt it fall on my head," cried Chicken Little. "And I heard it with my own ears!"

Turkey Lurkey thought this was just terrible! And so he joined Chicken Little and Henny Penny on their quest to tell the king. The trio ran down the road as fast as they could, and soon came upon Goosey Loosey.

"What's the matter?" Goosey Loosey asked the anxious birds.

"The sky is falling!" Turkey Lurkey gobbled. "Henny Penny told me."

"I heard it from Chicken Little," said Henny Penny.

"I felt it fall on my head," said Chicken Little. "I heard it with my own ears, and I saw it with my own eyes!"

"Golly!" said Goosey Loosey. "I always knew the sky would fall one day!"

"We're off to tell the king!" said Chicken Little.

"No time to chat!" Turkey Lurkey added. "Let's go!"

And so Goosey Loosey joined the group, honking loudly as she ran along.

Just then, Foxy Loxy stepped onto the road.

"Little birdies!" cried Foxy Loxy. "Where are you going in such a rush? What ever is the matter?"

"We're going to see the king," Goosey Loosey announced. "The sky is falling!"

"How do you know the sky is falling?" Foxy Loxy asked.

"Why, Turkey Lurkey told me!" Goosey Loosey replied. "He heard it from Henny Penny, who heard it from Chicken Little. And Chicken Little heard it with her own ears and saw it with her own eyes!"

Foxy Loxy looked up at the sky. It looked just like it always did, and certainly didn't seem to be falling. Besides, he could always take shelter in his den if it did start to crumble.

Sure that the sky was not falling, the sneaky fox decided to lure the birds to his den so he could eat them.

"Follow me, friends!" cried Foxy Loxy. "I will show you the way to a secret shortcut. It leads right into the castle courtyard, so you'll soon be able to warn the king."

And so the birds ran after Foxy Loxy, who led them to his den.

"Step through here," said Foxy Loxy. "Don't be afraid of the dark. Just follow the tunnel and you'll soon pop out the other end, right in the castle courtyard."

Chicken Little and the birds looked at each other nervously. They had to warn the king, but could they really trust Foxy Loxy?

Just then, the birds and the fox heard loud barking. The king's hounds were running across the field. The dogs were coming straight at them!

As the birds squawked and flapped their wings, Foxy Loxy bolted across the field. Tricking the birds wasn't worth being caught by the king's hounds!

The hounds sniffed the entrance of the fox's den. Then they sniffed Chicken Little and all her friends.

"What are you doing here?" asked one of the hounds.

"Please take us to see the king!" Chicken Little pleaded. "We must tell him that the sky is falling!"

The hounds had never heard of a sky falling. However, the king was a very smart man, so the hounds were sure he would know what to do.

The hounds led the fine-feathered friends back to the castle. The birds were brought before the king, who was curious to know why they had traveled so far.

"Hello, Chicken Little," said the king. "I've heard that you've traveled a great distance to see me."

"Oh, Your Majesty!" cried Chicken Little. "We've come to warn you that the sky is falling!"

"How do you know the sky is falling?" asked the king.

"I felt it fall on my head!" Chicken Little exclaimed. "I heard it with my own ears, and I saw it with my own eyes!"

"Where were you when this happened?" the king asked.

"I was walking past a big oak tree," Chicken Little replied. "Then it got really windy, and a piece of the sky fell on my head!"

"And did any other pieces of the sky fall on you as you traveled here?"

"No," Chicken Little replied.

"What about you?" the king asked Henny Penny. "Did you feel, see, or hear the sky fall?"

"No, Your Majesty," said Henny Penny. "I heard it from Chicken Little."

"And what about you?" the king asked the other birds.

"I heard it from Turkey Lurkey," said Goosey Loosey.

"And I heard it from Henny Penny," said Turkey Lurkey.

"Well," said the king. "It seems to me that the sky is not falling. In fact, there is a very simple explanation."

The birds twittered excitedly. They knew the king would figure out what was going on!

"It wasn't a piece of the sky that fell on your head," said the king. "It was merely an acorn!"

The birds couldn't believe it! Was all the panic really caused by a single acorn? They asked the king how he figured it out.

"Because Chicken Little was standing under an oak tree on a windy day!" the king replied.

The birds all laughed. They were so happy that the sky wasn't falling!

Before the birds went back home, the king gave Chicken Little an umbrella. From that day forward, she always carried the umbrella while she walked about. And if an acorn fell, Chicken Little didn't mind one bit!